The Gingerbread Boy

A Viking Easy-to-Read Classic

retold by **Harriet Ziefert**

illustrated by **Emily Bolam**

VIKING

VIKING
Published by the Penguin Group
Penguin Books USA Inc., 375 Hudson Street, New York, New York 10014, U.S.A.
Penguin Books Ltd, 27 Wrights Lane, London W8 5TZ, England
Penguin Books Australia Ltd, Ringwood, Victoria, Australia
Penguin Books Canada Ltd, 10 Alcorn Avenue, Toronto, Ontario, Canada M4V 3B2
Penguin Books (N.Z.) Ltd, 182–190 Wairau Road, Auckland 10, New Zealand

Penguin Books Ltd, Registered Offices: Harmondsworth, Middlesex, England

First published in the United States of America by Viking,
a division of Penguin Books USA Inc., 1995

Published simultaneously in Puffin Books

1 3 5 7 9 10 8 6 4 2

Text copyright © Harriet Ziefert, 1995
Illustrations copyright © Emily Bolam, 1995
All rights reserved

LIBRARY OF CONGRESS CATALOGING-IN-PUBLICATION DATA
Ziefert, Harriet.
The gingerbread boy / retold by Harriet Ziefert;
illustrated by Emily Bolam.   p.   cm.—(A Viking easy-to-read classic)
Summary: A freshly baked gingerbread boy escapes when he is taken out
of the oven and eludes his pursuers until he meets a clever fox.
ISBN 0-670-86052-2
[1. Fairy tales. 2. Folklore.]
I. Bolam, Emily, ill. II. Gingerbread boy. III. Title. IV. Series.
PZ8.Z54Gi 1995 398.21—dcE—dc20 95-19535 CIP AC

Printed in Hong Kong   Set in New Century Schoolbook

Viking® and Easy-to-Read® are registered trademarks of Penguin Books USA Inc.

Reading level 1.9

The Gingerbread Boy

A little old man and
a little old woman
lived in a little old house.

They had no children.

The little old woman
wanted a little boy.
So she made a boy
out of gingerbread.

Then she put him
in the oven to bake.

The little old woman
opened the oven door.

Out jumped the little
gingerbread boy and…

away he ran—out of
the little old house!
"Stop! Stop!"
said the little old woman.

"Stop! Stop!"
said the little old man.

But the little gingerbread
boy said:
"Run, run, as fast as you can.
You can't catch me—
I'm the gingerbread man!"

The little gingerbread boy
ran on and on.
He ran past a cow.
"Stop! Stop!"
said the cow.

But the little gingerbread
boy said:
"I have run away
from a little old woman
and a little old man.
I can run away from you—I can!"

The little gingerbread boy
ran on and on.
He ran past a horse.
"Stop! Stop!" said the horse.

But the little gingerbread
boy said:
"I have run away from
a little old woman,
a little old man, and a cow.
I can run away from you—I can!"

The little gingerbread boy
ran on and on.
He ran past a farmer.

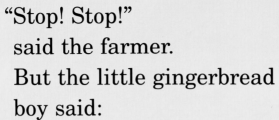

"Stop! Stop!"
said the farmer.
But the little gingerbread
boy said:

"I have run away from
a little old woman,
a little old man,
a cow, and a horse.
I can run away from you—I can!"

The little gingerbread boy
ran on and on until
he came to a river.
Then he stopped.

A fox was running by.
He saw the gingerbread boy.
He knew the gingerbread boy
would make a good snack.

The fox was smart.
He said to the gingerbread boy,
"I'll help you cross the river.
Sit on my tail."

The little gingerbread boy
sat on the fox's tail.

The fox began to swim
across the river.

"You're getting wet,"
said the fox.
"Why don't you jump
onto my back?"

The little gingerbread boy
jumped onto the fox's back.

Then the fox said:
"You are too heavy
to sit on my back.
Why don't you jump
onto my head?"

Then the fox said:
"You are still too heavy.
Why don't you jump
onto my nose?"

So the little gingerbread boy
jumped onto the fox's nose.

Then the fox turned
his head and...

Crunch! Munch!
Munch! Crunch!

The little gingerbread boy
was all gone!